make way for NODDY ™

Big Fun Storybook

Collins

An imprint of HarperCollinsPublishers

CONTENTS

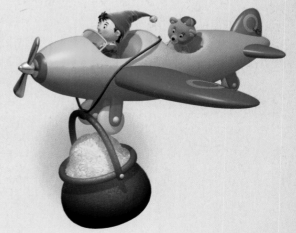

Noddy's Perfect Gift

It was a peaceful morning in Toy Town, until...

VROOM! Noddy's little yellow car roared up the road and screeched to a halt outside Toadstool House.

Noddy jumped out, pushed open the front door and dashed inside.

"Big-Ears! Big-Ears!" he shouted.

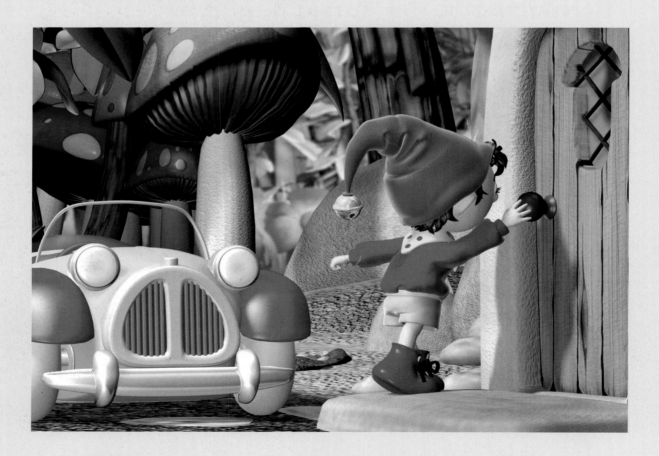

"It must be very important if you're in such a rush, Noddy," said Big-Ears. "What's the problem?"

"I don't know! I don't know! I don't know!"
cried Noddy, pacing up and down.

"Well, if you don't know what the problem is, how can I possibly help you?" said Big-Ears.

Noddy tried to explain.

"Oh, Big-Ears, I'm not sure if my birthday present for Tessie Bear is enough. It's just a song I made up."

"A song sounds like a lovely present, Noddy," said Big-Ears smiling. "Sing it and I'll tell you what I think."

Noddy cleared his throat and began to sing:
    This song is for your birthday, Tessie Bear, it's true.
    Yes, every note I've written is especially for you.
    I like you, Tessie Bear, you must know it's true.
    Friend of mine, every line shows how much I do.

"What do you think, Big-Ears?" Noddy asked. "Should it be longer? Shorter? Prettier?"

    "It's perfect just as it is, Noddy," said Big-Ears.

    "Are you sure, Big-Ears?" said Noddy.

    "She'll love it, Noddy," Big-Ears promised him. "Off you go, now! And don't come back until you've sung it to her."

Noddy set off to see Tessie Bear.

Suddenly someone called out, "Taxi! Taxi!"
It was Martha Monkey. Noddy pulled over.

"Sorry Martha, I can't give you a lift, I've got something very important to do!"

But Martha just jumped in. "Oh, please, Noddy, I need to get to Town Square."

"OK then," sighed Noddy.

"I hear it's Tessie Bear's birthday," said Martha, when they arrived in Toy Town. "Is she having a party? Who's invited? And, most important, what are you giving her?"

"A song! I made it up myself," said Noddy.

"A song is nice, I suppose," said Martha, "but it might not be enough to make her feel extra special."

Noddy looked worried again. Perhaps a song wasn't the best present, after all. "Oh, Martha," he cried. "What *would* make Tessie Bear feel extra special?"

"Flowers always make *me* feel special," said Martha giving him a wink.

"Of course! Flowers!" Noddy whooped happily. "Why didn't I think of that?"

Noddy was sure Tessie Bear would like the forget-me-nots he'd bought. They were just like the flowers on her hat.

"What lovely flowers," said Mr Wobbly Man.

"They're for Tessie Bear," Noddy told him proudly. "And I've made up a special birthday song for her."

"Lucky Tessie!" said Mr Wobbly Man. "But what about a cake? A cake is the best part of a birthday."

"Oh, no! I didn't think of that," wailed Noddy. "I've just got time to make one. Will you help me?"

Whirrrrrrrrr... went the mixing machine.

"Phew! Whipping up a cake is hard work," said Noddy.

"Let me taste it for you," said Mr Wobbly Man, scooping some of the creamy mixture into his mouth.

"Hmmm. This cake mixture needs a little more... tasting!" said Mr Wobbly Man and he gobbled it all up!

"Sorry, Noddy, you'll have to make another one," said Mr Wobbly Man.

"But I've only got enough eggs for a bite-sized cake, this time," moaned Noddy. "No more tasting, Mr Wobbly Man!" he said firmly, measuring more flour into his mixing bowl.

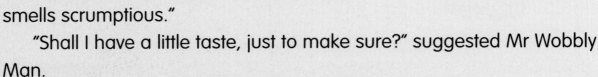

"Small but perfect," said Noddy proudly as he took the cake out of the oven. "And it smells scrumptious."

"Shall I have a little taste, just to make sure?" suggested Mr Wobbly Man.

"No!" cried Noddy, snatching the cake away. "I'm taking it to Tessie Bear, right now!"

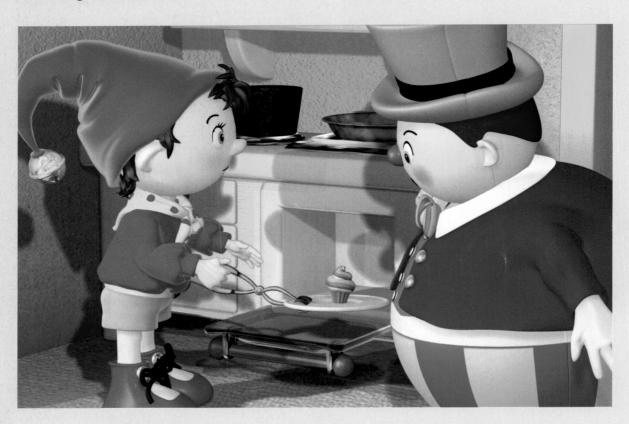

But Mr Wobbly Man started to groan. "Ooo, my tummy! I've eaten too much cake mixture."

Poor Noddy had to drive Mr Wobbly Man to the shop to get some medicine. Would he ever get to Tessie Bear's house?

As he came out of the shop, Noddy saw Sly and Gobbo, the two goblins, leaning over his car.

"Hey!" Noddy shouted. "What are you up to?"

The naughty goblins jumped back.

"We were, er... you tell him, Sly," said Gobbo.

"Me?" said Sly. "Oh, OK. We were trying to snatch –"

SLAP! Gobbo slapped a hand over Sly's mouth and hissed, "*Sniff* not *snatch*. We were just sniffing the pretty flowers. The cake smelt yummy, too."

Noddy rushed to his car. The cake and flowers were safe. "Those are my presents for Tessie's birthday," he told the goblins.

"Birthday presents, eh?" said Gobbo thoughtfully. "We can help with presents, can't we, Sly?"

And he yanked Sly aside to whisper to him. There was a lot of giggling and Sly kept nodding his head.

Finally, the two cheeky goblins turned back to Noddy. Gobbo said, "Sly and I think the best way to make Tessie Bear happy is to give her..."

"...some jelly!" sniggered Sly.

"No!" hissed Gobbo. "Jewellery!"

"Jewellery?" said Noddy, looking worried.

"Yes and we know where you can get it," said Gobbo.

"Step this way for some wonderful jewellery,"
said Gobbo, hurrying Noddy down a back street.

"Are you sure there's a jewellery shop here?" said Noddy,
wondering if he should trust them.

"Oh, yes," said Sly. "Look!"

"What? Where? In these boxes?" gasped Noddy.

"This box is full of jewellery," said Gobbo, trying not to giggle. "Look! You'll be surprised."

Noddy thought it might be a trick but he just couldn't help peeping into the box.

Quick as a flash, Sly and Gobbo pushed him in and shut the lid. Poor Noddy was trapped!

"Yep! He was surprised, all right," chortled Sly.

"Now for the great car snatch!" yelled Gobbo.

The goblins raced down the street and dived into Noddy's car.

Shrieking with laughter, they roared up and down the road, beeping the horn.

PARP! PARP!

And, to tease poor Noddy, they gave an extra loud beep every time they passed.

Thunk. Thunk. Thunk. The box bumped angrily down the street.

Then, just as Mr Plod walked by, the box suddenly jumped!

"Aghh!" the policeman shouted in surprise.

A loud knocking came from inside the box. Mr Plod crept closer to have a look.

All at once, the box burst open and up popped Noddy! He was very cross.

"Arrest them, Mr Plod," he cried. "They're stealing my car!"

"Who? What? Where?" gasped Mr Plod, looking all around.

Just then, the goblins came roaring down the road in Noddy's little car.

"Why, those scoundrels!" said Mr Plod.
He stepped into the road, raised his hand and blew a loud blast on his whistle.

"Peeeep! Stop in the name of Plod!" he commanded.
Gobbo braked hard. The little yellow car screeched to a halt, only just missing Mr Plod.

The two goblins bashed their noses on the windscreen. "Aghh! Ouch!" they groaned.

"You ought to be ashamed of yourselves, stealing Noddy's car like that," Mr Plod told them sternly.

"Sorry, Mr Plod," said Gobbo. "Sometimes our naughty side just runs away with us!"

"Yeah, like now!" yelled Sly. And the two naughty goblins leaped out of the car and ran away, hooting with laughter. Mr Plod raced off after them, blowing his whistle. Peeep-peep!

Poor Noddy. His cake and flowers were crushed to bits.
"What's the matter, Noddy?" asked Big-Ears, who was passing by.
"I wanted to give Tessie an extra-special birthday. But Sly and Gobbo have wrecked everything," cried Noddy.
"But what about your song? It came straight from your heart," said Big-Ears. "It's a perfect present!"
"You really think so?" said Noddy. And he rushed off to find Tessie.

This song is for your birthday, Tessie Bear, it's true.
Yes, every note I've written is especially for you.
I like you, Tessie Bear, you must know it's true.
Friend of mine, every line shows how much I do.

Noddy stopped singing and looked shyly at Tessie.
"Thank you, Noddy!" She beamed at him. "It's the most perfect
present I've ever had!"

Sing-a-Song
Spot the Difference

Noddy is singing his special song to Tessie.
Can you spot all six differences between the two pictures?
Sing Noddy's song when you have finished!

Make Way for Noddy (Noddy!)
He toots his horn to say
Make Way for Noddy (Noddy!)
Come on out and play

Make Way for Noddy (Noddy!)
Shout a big 'Hooray'
Let's get ready, and steady – GO!!
It's a happy day
Noddy's here
Make Way

green roof
no wall lamp

no lamp
blue skirt

blue flowers
one button on shirt

Birthday Count and Colour

Noddy has some lovely flowers for Tessie Bear.

Point to and count all these things in the picture!

How many red shoes?

How many blue hats?

How many red apples?

How many pink ribbons?

Noddy is thinking about ideas for Tessie's birthday present.
Colour all the things you like!

Bake a Cake with Noddy

Noddy is busy making a cake for Tessie.

Can you spot the **bowl, milk, eggs** and **flour**
Noddy needs to make the cake?
Tick the boxes when you've spotted them!

Can You Match the Shadows?

Here are Noddy and his
friends from the story.

28

Match each friend to their shadow by drawing a line.

The Magic Powder

It was a sparkling spring morning in Toy Town...

"Ahh! What lovely weather!" sighed Mr Sparks. "It makes you want to sing and dance, doesn't it, Noddy?"

"It certainly does! I – oh, my goodness!"

All of a sudden, Noddy slammed on the brakes and jerked the steering wheel.

SCREEEECH! Noddy's little car skidded wildly before coming to a standstill sideways across the road.

Mr Sparks grabbed hold of his hat. Noddy's head shook so hard his bell tinkled madly.

"W-w-what happened?" gasped Mr Sparks, looking very startled.

"Sorry, Mr Sparks," said Noddy. "Something leaped out in front of the car. I only just missed it – Oh!"

"*Woof-woof-woof*!" Two paws and an eager nose appeared over the top of the car door.

"It's Bumpy Dog!" cried Mr Sparks.
"And he's very happy to see you, Noddy!"
Bumpy barked and started licking Noddy's nose.
But Noddy wasn't very happy.
"Bumpy! I nearly crashed into you! Get DOWN!"
"Don't be too hard on him," said Mr Sparks.
"He's only a puppy. He doesn't understand about traffic rules."

Bumpy took a flying leap into the car.
But Noddy was still cross.
"You shouldn't run out in front of cars, Bumpy!" he scolded.
Bumpy Dog hung his head.

They were soon zooming along again towards Toy Town. Then, all of a sudden, Bumpy Dog jumped up at Noddy again.

"Get down at once, Bumpy!" shouted Noddy. "You should never, EVER mess about in a car!"

Bumpy whined. He hated it when Noddy was cross.

Poor Noddy. Something even worse was brewing in Dark Wood. The two bad goblins, Gobbo and Sly, were up to their usual tricks.

"Just two more things to add!" chortled Gobbo:

The sparkling laces of a ballerina's shoe,
The tapping rhythm of a drumstick true.
Dancing Potion, Dancing Potion,
Now you turn BLUE!

There was a FLASH! and the magic potion turned into sparkling blue powder.

Gobbo scooped up a handful. "Soon all of Toy Town will be dancing to our tune," he gloated.

"But Gobbo," whined Sly, "dancing's fun."

"They won't think it's fun when we've finished with them!" grinned Gobbo.

Soon Noddy stopped his car near Town Square.

"Thanks for the ride, Noddy," said Mr Sparks.

Bumpy was so excited that he jumped up again – and knocked Noddy over.

"Get DOWN!" Noddy cried. "Will you stop jumping and bumping all over the place?"

Poor Bumpy whined sadly and slunk away with his tail between his legs.

Just then, Noddy heard someone ringing a bell.

It was Gobbo the goblin.

"Roll up! Roll up!" yelled Gobbo. "Prepare to be AMAZED!"

What was Gobbo up to?

A crowd soon gathered to watch and Noddy joined them.

"No energy? Sore, aching feet?" cried Gobbo. "Never fear! I have here... a magic cure!"

And he waved towards a bottle full of sparkling blue powder.

"My Magic Comfort Foot Powder will put a spring in your step! You'll feel as if you're walking on air. One sprinkle and you'll be dancing in the streets!" Gobbo cried.

The Toy Town crowd murmured with surprise. Could they really trust Gobbo?

Just then, a stranger limped forward.

"Oooo, my feet are so-o-o sore," moaned the stranger. "I'd do anything to get rid of the pain."

"You won't be sorry, sir!" smirked Gobbo, as he pretended to sprinkle the powder over the stranger's feet.

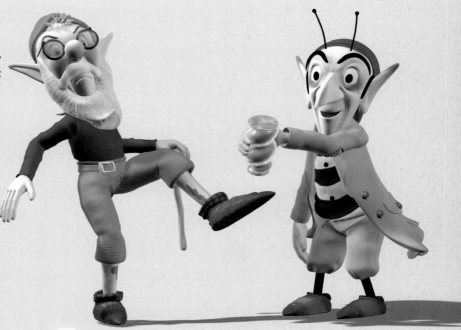

"Wow!" Everyone gasped as the stranger leaped into the air and danced wildly across the stage.

The amazing dance convinced everyone.

"How much is that magic powder?" called out Mr Plod, the policeman.

"It's free... for one day only!" grinned Gobbo.

"It sounds too good to be true," said Noddy. "But I'll try some."

Soon, everyone had a bottle of Gobbo's Magic Comfort Foot Powder and they sprinkled the sparkling blue powder over their feet.

"Ooo, it feels lovely!" sighed Dinah Doll.

"Like I'm floating on air!" laughed Noddy.

Mr Plod smiled at Gobbo, "You've done something good for a change! Thank you!"

"Only too happy to help!" smirked Gobbo as the crowd walked away. The stranger stayed behind.

"Can I take off my disguise now, Gobbo?" he asked. It was Sly!

Gobbo laughed. "Of course you can, Sly! Heh! Heh! They fell for our trick! All those silly people tried our magic foot powder. Now we just need a little tune!"

Sly turned the handle of their music box and a lively tune filled the air. All at once, the goblins' Magic Comfort Foot Powder began to work its magic.

Feet began tapping and heads began nodding as everyone broke into a wild, crazy dance, twirling and whirling and spinning all around the town.

The two naughty goblins roared with laughter.

"It's the funniest thing I've ever seen," gasped Sly.

"Now's our chance," said Gobbo. "They can't stop us stealing – they're too busy dancing!"

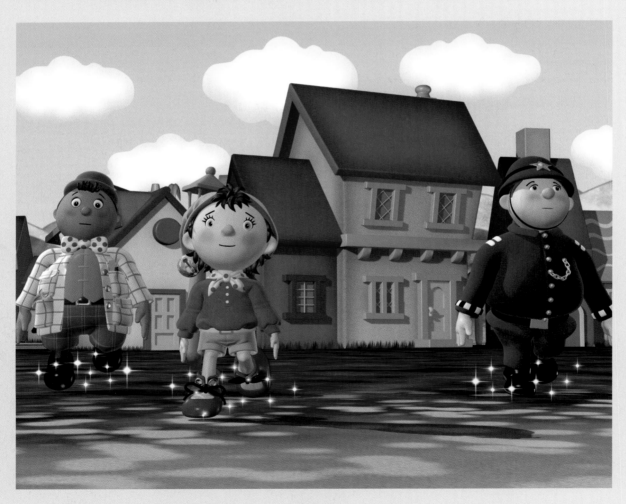

At Dinah Doll's stall, poor Dinah could only dance and scold as Gobbo filled his sack.

"Don't worry, Dinah, I'll arrest them!" cried Mr Plod, dancing towards the two goblins.

"Oh, no you won't!" Gobbo sniggered, as the music played even faster. Mr Plod could do nothing but dance, dance, dance!

"HELP!" he wailed, whirling down the street.

The goblins' music had set Noddy's feet dancing and his head nodding too.

"What a nice car!" said Gobbo as he climbed into Noddy's car.

"You leave my car alone!" cried Noddy angrily.

"What's that, Noddy?" sniggered Gobbo.

"Can't stop dancing? Never mind. We'll have your car."

The gleeful goblins loaded Noddy's car with everything they had stolen.

"There isn't one person in Toy Town who can stop us!" chortled Gobbo.

But he was wrong.

At that moment, Bumpy Dog wandered sadly into the square. But when he saw Noddy, he bounded happily up to him – and knocked him right over!

"Bumpy! Why aren't you dancing?" cried Noddy, his feet still dancing in the air.

Bumpy barked.

"Of course!" Noddy laughed. "You don't have any magic powder on your paws so you aren't under the spell!"

He hugged Bumpy. "Now, go and stop those goblins!"

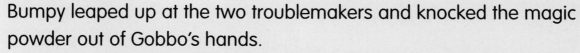

Bumpy leaped up at the two troublemakers and knocked the magic powder out of Gobbo's hands.

PUFF! A cloud of sparkling blue powder billowed out around them.

"Why, you pesky pooch, I'll – uh-oh!" Gobbo cried as his feet began to jiggle and wriggle.

Soon the two goblins were dancing furiously.

"Quick! Stop the music, Sly!" Gobbo shouted.

Sly stopped the music box and the goblins stopped dancing. But so did everyone else.

"Stop, in the name of Plod!" shouted the policeman as he ran towards them.

"Oops!" cried Gobbo. "You'd better start playing again, Sly!"

CRASH! Bumpy Dog knocked the music box out of Sly's hand and it smashed to pieces.

"Let's get out of here!" cried Gobbo.

But it was too late!

Mr Plod grabbed both goblins.

"Going somewhere?" he asked sternly.

"Heh, heh. To jail?" Sly said helpfully.

"You guessed it!" said Mr Plod.

"Well done, Bumpy, you're a hero!" said Dinah. "You deserve that bone for saving us from those naughty goblins."

"You're a great dog, Bumpy," cried Mr Sparks.

Then Bumpy bounded up to Noddy, wagging his tail like mad.

"I'm sorry I was mean to you, Bumpy," said Noddy. "Without all your jumping and bumping, we'd still be dancing to the goblins' tune! Are we still friends?"

Bumpy barked, leaped up at Noddy and... knocked him off his feet.

"Oh, Bumpy!" laughed Noddy.

Magical Maze

Help Bumpy Dog find his way to the naughty goblins and their magic powder!

Double Trouble!

Noddy has been trying out one of Big-Ear's magic spells.
He's made everything double!

Match up all the pairs by drawing lines
so that Noddy can fix the spell.

Naughty Goblins

The naughty goblins are up to mischief.
Can you spot 6 differences between the two pictures?

one button on jacket
blue trousers

one antennae
one pink eye

one green shoe
no arm

"Stop, in the name of Plod!"

Which of these make a noise?
Point to it and make the sound.

Colour Mr. Plod with your pencils, pens or crayons.

Noddy on the Move

It was a sunny day in Toy Town and Noddy and Master Tubby Bear were in Noddy's little House-for-One.

"I wish we could go somewhere exciting," said Master Tubby Bear.

"Me, too!" said Noddy.

"But we never go anywhere," said Master Tubby Bear, sadly.

Noddy looked out of the window.

"But we can!" he grinned. "I can move house!"

Master Tubby Bear was very upset.

"But Noddy! You can't leave Toyland," he cried.

"I won't leave Toyland," explained Noddy, laughing. "I'll go and live in another part of Toyland. I could live near the Ice-Cream Parlour –"

Tubby Bear smiled, "– and then you'd get ice-cream every day!"

Noddy was so excited, he couldn't wait to find a new place to live.

"Will you help me, Tubby Bear?" he cried.

"Oh, yes!" said Tubby Bear.

"It's moving day for Noddy!"

Big-Ears was cycling peacefully down the road when he heard the sound of Noddy's car.

Big-Ears couldn't believe his eyes.

Noddy was pulling his little House-for-One along on wheels.

"I'm moving!" said Noddy, proudly.

"But, Noddy!" cried Big-Ears. "What's wrong with where you used to live?"

"Boring!" laughed Noddy. "Now I'm going to find the PERFECT place."

And he roared off down the road.

"Hm," said Big-Ears, thoughtfully. "The perfect place, eh? I wonder!"

Noddy was so excited at the idea of moving that he couldn't help singing:

> *Watch how I move*
> *My House-for-One.*
> *Life will improve,*
> *Moving is fun!*

Noddy and Tubby Bear went to tell Tessie Bear all about their moving plans.

"Why don't you live next door to me, Noddy?" said Tessie. "Then we can have tea together every day. We can feed my chickens – that's funny. Where ARE my chickens? They were here a moment ago."

Noddy and Tessie Bear hunted everywhere. But the chickens had completely vanished.

Then Master Tubby Bear opened the door of Noddy's little house.

"Here they are," he cried. "And they're making a terrible mess!"

"What can I do!" cried Noddy.

"You've put your house where they live," said Tessie Bear. "So they think it's THEIR house."

"But I don't want to live in a chicken house!" said poor Noddy.

"It's no good, Tessie," said Noddy, sadly. "I shall have to move."

Master Tubby Bear and Noddy
climbed into Noddy's little car and set
off again. But Noddy soon cheered
up and he began to sing:

> I'll find a spot
> Meant to be mine.
> I'll smile a lot,
> Moving is fine.

"There's Mr Sparks' garage," said
Tubby Bear.

"Why don't you live next door to Mr Sparks?"

"What a good idea!" said Noddy. "I'd love to have him as a neighbour. He's so good at fixing things!"

Noddy and Tubby Bear had just parked Noddy's house, when all of sudden, there was a terrific noise.

BOOM-BOOM-WHHEEEE-OOOO!! Noddy's house bounced up and down.

"What is T-H-A-T?" cried Noddy.

"It's Mr Sparks, working in his garage," said Master Tubby Bear.

Noddy looked a bit worried.

"I expect I'll get used to it," he said. But he couldn't help thinking how nice and quiet it was where he lived before. Then they heard the sound of a horn. PAARP!

"What's happening?" said Master Tubby Bear. Noddy ran to the door and looked out.

There was Mr Sparks in his big tow truck.

"Oh, Mr Sparks!" cried Noddy. "I'm your new neighbour!"

"But Noddy!" cried Mr Sparks. "Your house is in the way! I can't get out of my garage!"

"I'm sorry, Mr Sparks," cried Noddy.

"We'll just have to move," said Master Tubby Bear. "Right away!"

"Never mind... We'll soon find the perfect place," said Noddy. "What about Town Square?"

"Why didn't we think of that before?" said Tubby Bear. "You'll see your friends every day. Everyone goes to Town Square."

Noddy was very happy. "It's going to be perfect!" he cried.

Noddy and Tubby Bear were looking out of the window at Town Square.

All of a sudden, there was a knock at Noddy's front door.

"My first visitor!" he said. "I wonder who it is?"

It was Mr Jumbo. He walked straight in.

And before Noddy and Master Tubby Bear could say a word, he took out a picnic hamper and began to unpack it.

"Mr Jumbo!" said Noddy, amazed.

"What are you doing?"

"I have a picnic on this spot in Town Square, every day," he said. "And now your house is here, I shall have to sit on your floor!"

"Oh," said Noddy, "I suppose so."

Perhaps Town Square wasn't going to be such a good idea, after all!

Just then, they heard loud, squeaky giggles getting closer and closer.

"Who's that?" said Tubby Bear.

CRASH!

A crowd of blue, green and pink Bouncy Balls whizzed into Noddy's little house and started bouncing all over it.

"Didn't you know?" said Mr Jumbo. "The Bouncy Balls practise bouncing here in Town Square, every day."

"But I live here, now," said poor Noddy.

"That's not going to stop the Bouncy Balls," said Mr Jumbo.

"NODDY!" shouted a voice.

Oh, dear! More trouble. It was Mr Plod.

Noddy opened his door.

"Move in the name of Plod!" said the policeman, sternly. "Town Square is a no-house-parking-zone!"

Noddy looked at Mr Jumbo, spilling crumbs on his clean floor. He looked at the Bouncy Balls, whizzing in and out of his windows. And he looked at Mr Plod's cross face.

"All right," he said. "I really wanted somewhere a bit less CROWDED…"

But it wasn't that easy. Everywhere seemed to be full up.

Some time later, Big-Ears met a very tired Noddy and Tubby Bear driving down the road.

"Still moving house?" asked Big-Ears.

"We've been moving ALL DAY!" said Noddy. "But there were too many chickens and too much noise."

"And too many Bouncy Balls," said Tubby Bear.

Big-Ears thought for a moment.

"I do know somewhere you could try," he suggested. "A very pretty place. With no chickens. And no Bouncy Balls, either."

Wearily, Noddy and Master Tubby Bear followed Big-Ears. And a few minutes later they arrived…

They were back exactly where Noddy had always lived!
"Oh, Big-Ears!" laughed Noddy. "It's the best place in the world."
"Are you sure?" said Master Tubby Bear.
"I've been moving all day," smiled Noddy.
"And I know now that this place is PERFECT!"

Chicken Chase

Noddy is trying to catch Tessie Bear's chickens.
Can you help him count them all?

Well done, you helped him count 10 chickens.
Use your pencils, pens and crayons to colour Noddy.

Match the Bouncy Balls

There are 10 Bouncy Balls!
Can you match them up into pairs
before they bounce away?

73

House-for-One
Spot the Difference

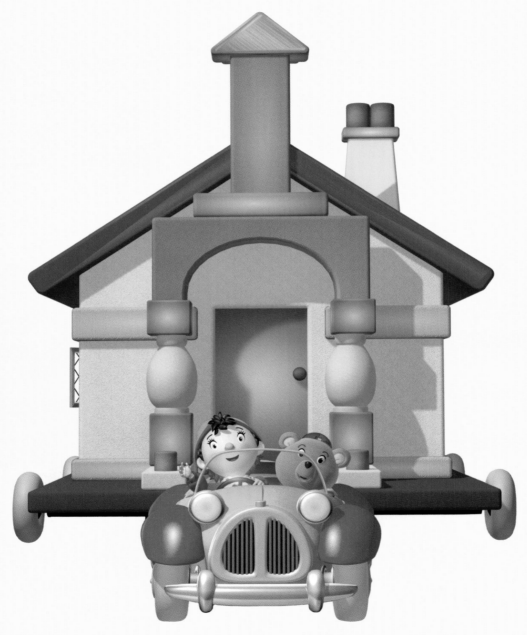

Noddy is on the move!
Can you spot six differences between the pictures?

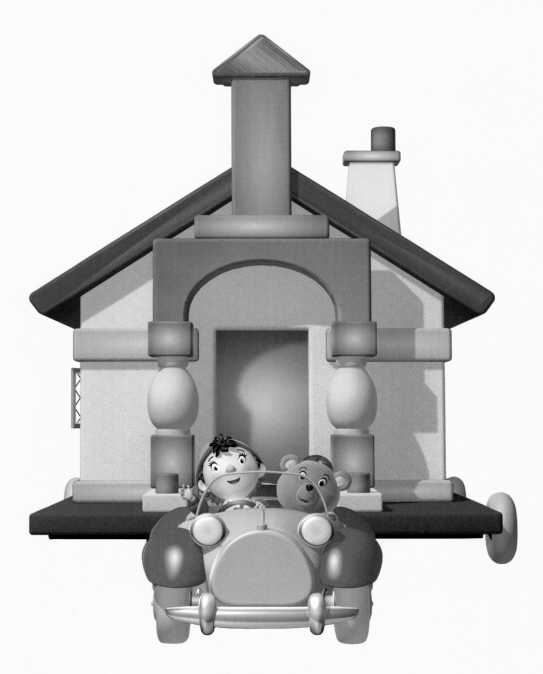

red triangle top
blue arch

one chimney pot
no door knob

no car grill
no front wheel to carrier

Noddy and Friends
Colouring Fun

Noddy is happy to
see all his friends!
Colour them with your
pencils, pens and crayons.

Noddy and the Magic Bagpipes

It was a chilly day in Toyland...

Big-Ears and Noddy were playing a game in Toadstool House. Noddy was puzzling over his next move, when Big-Ears wanted a warm rug. Noddy leaped up. "I'll get it!" he said.

BLARRRRP!

"Agghh!" gasped Noddy. "There's a monster in your cupboard, Big-Ears!"

Big-Ears strode towards the cupboard.

"Ooooh! Be careful, Big-Ears," Noddy warned him. "It sounds very angry."

Big-Ears reached into the cupboard.

BLARRRRP!

Noddy jumped back in horror.

Big-Ears chuckled. "Don't be scared, Noddy," he said. "That's not a monster. That's my bagpipes. I can play music on them. Listen."

Big-Ears took a big, deep breath and blew into the bagpipes. His fingers danced over the holes and the bagpipes let out a loud *wagh-wagh-wagh* tune.

"What a wonderful sound!" sighed Noddy, dreamily. How magical it would be if he could play the bagpipes!

"Will you teach me to play?" Noddy asked.
"It takes a lot of time and practise to play the bagpipes, Noddy," Big-Ears warned.
"But I really want to learn. Please teach me, Big-Ears," Noddy begged.

Big-Ears looked serious. "These are special bagpipes, Noddy," he said. "They need a lot of care. And you must practise. You have to play them every day."

"Yes, yes, I'll do it," agreed Noddy. "I'll work really hard, Big-Ears, I promise."

Big-Ears smiled as they got ready for Noddy's first lesson.

"Let's start now," whooped Noddy.

"I'll teach you a simple tune," said Big-Ears. "Then you must practise it every single day. Understand?"

"Yes, Big-Ears," said Noddy, eagerly. "I'll practise first thing, every day."

Next morning, Noddy leaped out of bed.
He wrestled the bagpipes into position, took a
big, deep breath and blew.

BLARRRPP-RRRNNNNN-SSSSSHHH!

"That didn't sound anything like the tune
Big-Ears played," grumbled Noddy. "I'll try
again."

And he took another big, deep breath.

But just as Noddy was about to blow into
the pipes, he saw his yellow kite leaning
against the wall.

"There's a perfect breeze today. I think
I'll fly my kite," said Noddy, throwing the
bagpipes on to the chair. "I can always practise tomorrow."

Next morning, Noddy was just about to start practising, when he heard Mr Sparks' voice.

"Hey, Noddy! Do you want to come fishing?"

"Sorry! I'm rather busy," Noddy called down.

Then he saw Mr Sparks' fishing rod.

"I can always practise the bagpipes tomorrow," Noddy said to himself. And again, he dropped them on the chair.

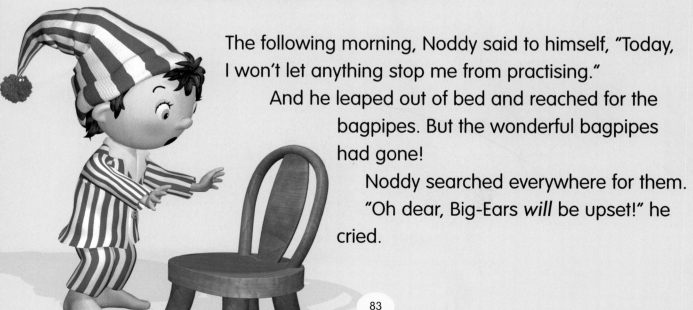

The following morning, Noddy said to himself, "Today, I won't let anything stop me from practising."

And he leaped out of bed and reached for the bagpipes. But the wonderful bagpipes had gone!

Noddy searched everywhere for them.

"Oh dear, Big-Ears *will* be upset!" he cried.

Down at his garage, Mr Sparks was busy working on a car.

The bagpipes crept up quietly beside him and... BLARRRP!

"Yahhhhh!" Mr Sparks jumped back and clunked his head. "What was THAT?" he wondered, looking up and down the empty street.

In the square, Dinah Doll was putting the last building block on a tower.

"There," she said, happily. "Now everyone will notice my stall."

BLARRRP! The cheeky bagpipes gave poor Dinah such a fright, she tumbled off her ladder.

"Whoaaaahh!" she yelled as she fell in a shower of blocks.

Dinah Doll and Mr Sparks were telling Mr Plod what had happened, when Noddy ran up to them.

"Mr Plod, there's been a bagpipes robbery!"

"Bagpipes, eh?" said Mr Plod. "I've just heard about a mysterious musical instrument on the loose in Toy Town."

BLARRRP! BLARRRP! BLARRRP!

"Listen!" cried Noddy. "It's the bagpipes."

Just at that moment, there was a clattering sound and Noddy and his friends looked round. But all they saw was a blur of tartan as the bagpipes dashed past.

WHEEEET! Mr Plod blew his whistle.

"Stop in the name of Plod!" he ordered, but the bagpipes took no notice and ran on, whining and wailing.

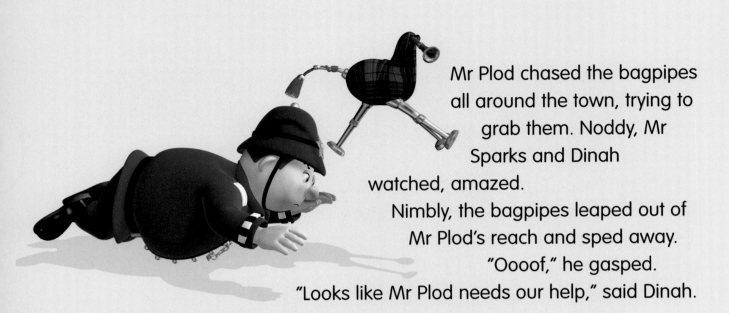

Mr Plod chased the bagpipes all around the town, trying to grab them. Noddy, Mr Sparks and Dinah watched, amazed.

Nimbly, the bagpipes leaped out of Mr Plod's reach and sped away.

"Oooof," he gasped.

"Looks like Mr Plod needs our help," said Dinah.

But the cheeky bagpipes leaped up at Dinah and Mr Sparks, and then clattered away as they tumbled over backwards.

"Ouch!" they both cried.

"Come back here, you!" shouted Noddy.

But the bagpipes took no notice.

Noddy ran round and round after the bagpipes, until he was dizzy.

"Now where has that pesky thing gone?" he wondered. BLAARRRP!

Noddy looked up. Perched on a branch were the bagpipes. He grabbed one of the dangling pipes and pulled.

"Got you!" he yelled.

Noddy held on tight, but the bagpipes began to grow bigger and bigger.

Suddenly, they let out a loud BLARRP! and took off. They were flying!

"Help! Help!" Noddy shouted, clinging on to the whooshing bagpipes.

As Noddy swooped past, Mr Plod grabbed hold of his feet. But Mr Plod was swept up into the air as well!

"Aghhh!" he gasped.

Then Mr Sparks grabbed on to Mr Plod's legs and Dinah grabbed Mr Sparks' legs.

But the clever bagpipes swooped down under a park bench – and zoomed out the other side without them.

That night, the bagpipes' non-stop wailing kept the whole of Toy Town awake.

Noddy gave up trying to sleep.

"I have to catch those bagpipes," he groaned.

Suddenly, Noddy heard a loud knocking on his door. Perhaps it was the bagpipes? He jumped out of bed.

"Big-Ears!" cried Noddy, as he opened the door.

"You didn't practise, did you?" said Big-Ears, crossly. "I warned you those bagpipes had to be played every day."

"I'm sorry, Big-Ears. I *did* mean to," Noddy said sadly.

He looked so upset that Big-Ears sighed, "Don't worry, Noddy. I just get grumpy when I'm tired."

"But why are the bagpipes running around screeching?" asked Noddy. "And keeping us all awake?"

"Magic," explained Big-Ears. "These bagpipes get restless if they're not played every day. They just want to make music – but they need help... which gives me an idea, Noddy!"

"A-one, a-two, a-three," said Big-Ears to his brand new band in Toy Town park.

BUZZ-BUZZ-BUZZ went Dinah on the kazoo.

WHEET-WHEET went Mr Plod on his whistle.

BOOM-BOOM went Mr Sparks on an oil drum.

And Noddy sang:

The best thing about this simple song
Is that anyone can play along...

The bagpipes watched the band. Then they leaped on to Noddy's chair.

Scooping them on to his lap, Noddy took a big, deep breath and blew. *Wagh-wagh-wagh*...

The bagpipes were happy now that they were making music in a real band.

And Noddy played every note perfectly.

"Wonderful!" said Big-Ears. "Our music has tamed the bagpipes!"

"But I think you ought to give them back to Big-Ears for safe-keeping, Noddy," said Mr Sparks.

"Yes," said Noddy. "You'd better have the bagpipes, Big-Ears. I might not practise every day!"

"OK, Noddy," said Big-Ears, smiling. "But first, let's play our tune just one more time."

"Right!" said Noddy, and took a big, deep breath.

And the new Toy Town band gave one last wonderful performance.

The best thing about this simple song
Is that anyone can play along.
Listen to the tune, and feel the beat,
Then clap your hands and stamp your feet!

Magical Musical Maze

The cheeky bagpipes have run away! Help Noddy find his way through the maze to fetch them. Say hello to Mr Plod and Big-Ears along the way.

"Let's play our tune just one more time!"

Now that Noddy can play the bagpipes
Big-Ears wants to hear the tune again!

Point to all these things in the pictures.

Tick the boxes when you have found them.

☐ flower	☐ shoe	☐ duck
☐ button	☐ window	☐ apple
☐ scarf	☐ leaf	

Match the Shadows

Can you match these
pictures from the story
to their shadows on the
other page?

Colour Fun!

Use your crayons to brighten up these pictures!

Noddy the Rainbow Chaser

It was a special day in Toy Town. A magic rainbow was sparkling in the sky over Town Square. Everyone was very excited.

"It's so beautiful!" cried Tessie
Bear. "Look at the yellow."

"Look at the orange," mewed Miss Pink Cat.

"And this red!" said Mr Wobbly Man.

"I love all the colours!" smiled Noddy. "But it hasn't rained. So
where has this rainbow come from?"

"It's a magic rainbow,
Noddy," said Big-Ears. "So it
doesn't need rain. It just turns
up when it feels like it."

"And makes everyone
happy," added Miss Pink Cat.
"I know, because it's been coming
ever since I was a Pink Kitten!"

Just then, the naughty goblins arrived. "Huh! Happy!" sneered Gobbo. "Who cares? There's a big pot of gold at the end of that rainbow."

"And when we find it WE'LL be happy!" said Sly. "Cos we'll be RICH!"

"Oh, no you won't!" said Mr Plod. "Because you're going to the police station, right now. Miss Pink Cat tells me you've been after her pies again!" And he whisked the grumbling goblins away.

Noddy looked thoughtful.

"Oh, Noddy!" said Master Tubby Bear. "Do you really believe that story about the pot of gold?"

"Come with me, Tubby Bear," grinned Noddy. "I've just had a brilliant idea!"

Noddy took Master Tubby Bear to find the Toy Town plane.

"The goblins were right about one thing. It WOULD be nice to have all that gold," said Tubby Bear.

"That's why we're going on a treasure hunt – at the end of the magic rainbow!" said Noddy.

And Noddy sang a song:

>Each of us would have a golden house
>'Neath a silver tree.
>What great fun for you and me
>To be as rich as rich can be.

"So what are we waiting for? Let's follow that rainbow!"

It didn't take the friends long to get ready and soon they were in the air.

"I can't WAIT to get that treasure," sighed Master Tubby Bear, happily.

But then Noddy saw where the rainbow was leading them… To the Dark Wood!

"Maybe I don't want that gold, after all," said Master Tubby Bear.

But Noddy wouldn't give up so easily. He landed the plane right in the middle of Dark Wood!

"Follow me!" said Noddy, bravely.

Shimmering in the darkness, the magic rainbow stretched straight ahead. But fierce eyes winked at them through the gloom.

"I don't like this ONE BIT," grumbled Master Tubby Bear, running after his friend.

Suddenly, there it was. The end of the rainbow. And there, on top of a hillock was a pot full of glittering GOLD!

"WE'VE FOUND THE TREASURE!" yelled Noddy.

And the friends did a little dance for joy.

But then Noddy had a scary thought.

"Wait! Maybe there is a magic spell protecting the pot of gold. We'd better watch out!" he said.

All of a sudden, Tubby Bear felt someone tap him on the back.

"Is that you behind me, Noddy?" he quavered.

"I'm IN FRONT of you," said Noddy. "How can it be me?"

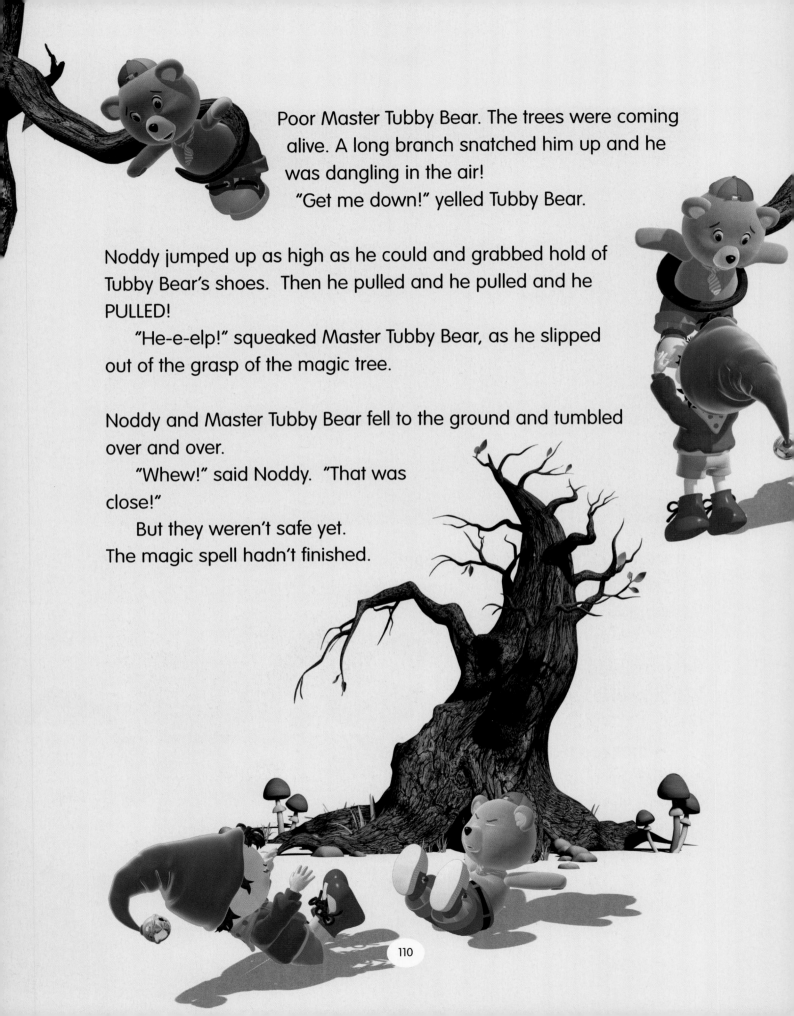

Poor Master Tubby Bear. The trees were coming alive. A long branch snatched him up and he was dangling in the air!

"Get me down!" yelled Tubby Bear.

Noddy jumped up as high as he could and grabbed hold of Tubby Bear's shoes. Then he pulled and he pulled and he PULLED!

"He-e-elp!" squeaked Master Tubby Bear, as he slipped out of the grasp of the magic tree.

Noddy and Master Tubby Bear fell to the ground and tumbled over and over.

"Whew!" said Noddy. "That was close!"

But they weren't safe yet.
The magic spell hadn't finished.

A magic storm whistled through the trees and whirled them up into the air.

Round and round they tossed until the wind blew them back into Noddy's plane.

"Now I AM giving up," said Noddy. "Let's go home!"

"But the treasure's just underneath us, Noddy," said Master Tubby Bear.

Noddy looked down from his plane and a very daring idea came into his head.

"Let's SCOOP it up, then. With the plane!"

Noddy was a good pilot and he held the plane steady as it roared over the Dark Wood.

Closer and closer they got to the pot of gold until Master Tubby Bear could drop a rope to grab hold of it.

"We've GOT THE GOLD!" whooped
Noddy. Then, all of a sudden, the
magic rainbow disappeared.

"Where did it go?" asked Master Tubby
Bear.

"I don't know," said Noddy. "But one thing I DO know. Everyone is
going to be very happy with us back in Toy Town!"

Everyone thought Noddy and Master
Tubby Bear had been so brave.

"They're heroes!" cried Miss Pink
Cat.
Noddy smiled proudly, but Big-Ears
frowned.

"Did the rainbow disappear when
you took the pot of gold?" he asked.

Noddy nodded.

    "Oh, dear!" said Big-Ears sadly. "That gold was put there by magic. It's what made the rainbow sparkle. Now it has been taken away, our wonderful rainbow has vanished for ever."

It was as if a big
grey cloud had settled
on Toy Town.
Everyone felt terrible.

"Oh, no!" sniffed Tessie
Bear. "I loved all those
beautiful colours!"

"So did I," sighed Mr
Wobbly Man.

"Don't be SAD!" cried Noddy. "I'll buy everyone
an ice-cream!"

"I just want our rainbow back,"
said Tessie Bear.

"Oh, Big-Ears!" cried Noddy. "What can I do?"
"There is one thing you can do," said Big-Ears
and he whispered in Noddy's ear.

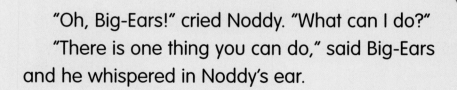

Soon afterwards, Noddy and Tubby Bear were in the plane again – only this time, they were taking the pot of gold BACK to the Dark Wood.

The second that the pot hit the ground, the magic rainbow sprang back into the air, sparkling more brightly than ever over Toy Town.

"We've done it, Tubby Bear," laughed Noddy and now I think we both deserve an ice-cream, don't you?"
And MasterTubby Bear had to agree.

Follow the Rainbows

Which rainbow will lead
Noddy and Master Tubby
Bear to the pot of gold?

Twice as Nice

Noddy and Tubby have decided they'll buy two of everything when they are rich with lots of gold!

Help them match up all the pairs.

Time for Tea

Noddy and Tubby have had a busy day!

Now they are very hungry.
Draw a circle around all the things they can eat!

Count along with Noddy!

Count all the way up
to 10 with Noddy.

1 apple

2 paint pots

5 ribbons

8 pencils

9 butterflies

3 birds

4 balloons

6 flowerpots

7 cakes

10 cups